CHILDREN'S TV
D0367931
SAM & MARK
LONG ARM
Vs
THE EVIL SUPPLY TEACHER
SCHOLASTIC
ILLUSTRATED BY ALEKSEI BITSKOFF

Scholastic Children's Books
An imprint of Scholastic Ltd
Euston House, 24 Eversholt Street, London, NW1 1DB, UK
Registered office: Westfield Road, Southam, Warwickshire, CV47 0RA
SCHOLASTIC and associated logos are trademarks and/or
registered trademarks of Scholastic Inc.
First published in the UK by Scholastic Ltd, 2016

ISBN 978 1407 15699 6

A CIP catalogue record for this book
is available from the British Library.

Printed by CPI Group (UK) Ltd, Croydon, CR0 4YY
Papers used by Scholastic Children's Books are made
from wood grown in sustainable forests.

1 3 5 7 9 10 8 6 4 2

www.scholastic.co.uk

Thank you to you reading this now.
We hope it fits nicely on your bookshelf. And if you don't have a bookshelf we hope it sits nicely on the window ledge in your bathroom next to the toilet ... and if you don't have a toilet then maybe you should have bought a toilet before you went and bought this book.

Welcome to *The Wolvesley Hour*. I'm Sammy Sammerson. Our top headlines for this evening…
Who is Long Arm?
Where did he come from?
And how can he possibly find sleeves that fit?
WHO IS LONG ARM?
HEADLINES TODAY
WHO IS LONG ARM?
ID HE COME FROM? AND HOW CAN HE POSSI

You're listening to Wolvesley FM where we guarantee to make your ears smile. I'm Clare Waves. Coming up on to 's show we'll be chatting about this long-armed crusader who's the talk of the town. That's coming up right after the new one from the Desert Penguins... It's out now and it's called 'It's a little too hot here'.

THE DAILY REFLECTION

Looking back at you, Wolvesley, every day!

LONG ARM STATUE UNVEILED BY MAYOR

Britain's Got Flatulence contestant Sharon: "I didn't expect it to smell that bad."

Full story page 5.

Wolvesley Zoo reports more missing animals. Head keeper says: "It makes no sense."

Full story page 9.

LongArm_WFC
Long Arm Superfan and Wolvesley FC supporter

WOLVESLEY TRENDS

#LongArm
62.7K Tweets in the last hour

#LongArmrescuespuppy
85.2K Tweets

#LongArmMonday
Trending for 3 hours now

#BGF
151K Tweets

#DesertPenguinsontour
49.4K Tweets

#WolvesleyFC
20.5K Tweets

#OrangeAdeHealthWarning
Just started trending

Sammy
Can you
saved ar
#LongAr

1.2

7.5

5.3

Trish<3
#LongAr
#LongAr

783

1.1

745

RealMa
Go #Lon

456

4.1

984

MaceyM
Another
#LongAr

News
LIVE
TV
WHO IS
1 ONE
SHOW
NEWS TV

TV

СОБЫТИЯ
ИНФОРМАЦИОННАЯ ПРОГРАММА

LONG ARM???

电视

TIME NOW

CHAPTER 1
A DOZY SUPERHERO

“Wake up, Mitre!” shouted his teacher, Mr Pinkerton.

Ricky sat bolt upright, his mind a mess. “What? Yes, Mummy. Coming!”

The class laughed, and Ricky blushed. Even Simon, Ricky’s best friend, was grinning.

"Sorry, sir," said Ricky. "I must have dozed off."

Mr Pinkerton was holding a stack of papers and his knuckles whitened. His face twisted into a frown, like an angry letter being screwed up.

"Children falling asleep in lessons" was a long way down Mr Pinkerton's List of Favourite Things (L.O.F.T). Let's take a look shall we?

L.O.F.T #1,233 - Children enjoying lessons

L.O.F.T #1,234 - Children falling asleep in lessons

L.O.F.T #1,235 - Children

"Dozing! DOZING? In maths!"

He said it as though dozing in maths was impossible. But Ricky didn't hear, because he'd fallen asleep again.

Mr Pinkerton slammed the papers down on to Ricky's desk. "Eyes open!" he yelled.

His face went pink. Then red. Then blue. It turned a shade of purple that frankly wasn't natural.

And when Mr Pinkerton's face goes THAT colour, there's no going back.

Ricky knew what was coming next. The whole class knew. You at home with this book in your hands, you know. Heck, even the aliens living on the planet Skidillybop probably have a good idea. A trump, a bottom burp. Or, if you're posh, a "breaking wind".

"Pinker-pump alert!" said Vince. "Activate defensive measures!"

But Mr Pinkerton took deep breaths, and performed a series of stretches like a yoga master.

"Flatulence averted!" he mumbled.

The entire class was shocked. It was unlike Mr Pinkerton to hold in a good trump. He always took immense pleasure in releasing his foul-smelling gas into the atmosphere. One time he let out a trump on every step he took leading up to the school library – all fifty-two of them. Nobody else visited the library that day.

Whatever the reason, everyone was grateful, including the aliens.

"He should be careful," Simon whispered to Ricky. "I've read that people can spontaneously combust from a build-up of methane. One spark, and BOOM!"

Ricky chuckled, but cut his chuckle short when Mr Pinkerton laid his latest test paper down on the desk. It had been graded W.

"What does W mean, sir?"

"Worse-Than-Even-I-Expected," replied Mr Pinkerton. "Which is *very* bad indeed."

"Ouch," muttered Simon.

"Double-Ouch," said Mr Pinkerton, giving Simon his test paper. Ricky saw Simon's face go pale as a flour-dusted sheet. His mouth opened in sheer horror.

He began to tremble uncontrollably.

"Are you OK?" said Ricky. "What did you get?"

Simon seemed to have lost the ability to speak, so Ricky peered over his shoulder. His paper was marked with an A.

"What's the matter?" asked Ricky. "An A is amazing."

"My parents are going to kill me," said Simon. "I've never got below an A+ before now."

Ricky was a bit disappointed though. Normally he got Cs. One time he thought he'd got a C+, but it turned out the "+" was just a bit of Pinkerton's curried egg that had fallen on to the paper.

But a W . . . that was definitely Worse-Than-Even-Ricky-Expected.

The problem? Well, being a superhero was tiring. Since Ricky's arm had stretched miraculously long in a hideous toilet-cleaning accident*, he'd been busy. Between completing the final levels of **Barry the Hedgehog** (his new favourite computer game), basketball practice and saving the world, Ricky didn't have a lot of time for maths revision. Still, if they asked, he would just tell his parents that the W stood for "Winner".

* It's pretty disgusting, but if you like that sort of thing, read *The Adventures of Long Arm*.

Mr Pinkerton had finished handing out the rest of the papers. "Anyone below an F, you'll be doing lines at break time."

Ricky put up his hand. "Is a W below an F?"

Mr Pinkerton rolled his eyes. "Yes, Ricky. Don't you know your alphabet either?" He turned to the board and wrote: *Mathematics nourishes the mind.* "Thirty times please, Ricky."

The bell went for assembly, and everyone scrambled up from their desks. On the way past, the class bully Vince bashed into Ricky. "Sorry, Mitre," he said. "Didn't see you down there."

The school hall was already filling up when Ricky's class arrived, so the only place left to sit was right at the front, in what was known as Spittle Row, because of head teacher Mrs Wilson's over-active saliva glands.

"Oh, great," said Vince, sliding on yesterday's outpouring. "I haven't brought my umbrella. Or a wetsuit."

Ricky found a dry spot on the floor and sat down. Simon pushed a button on the side of his thick spectacles, and a full-face visor slotted down. Typical Simon – always prepared.

But it wasn't Mrs Wilson who came into the hall. Instead, it was a youngish woman dressed head-to-toe in leathers, with a motorcycle helmet under her arm. She unzipped the leather jacket and tossed it on to the stage. Underneath she wore a T-shirt that read *Schoolz Out For Summer.*

"Who's that?" Katie Locke muttered, wide-eyed.

"Hi, guys!" said the woman, smiling brightly. "I'm afraid I have some bad news about Mrs Wilson."

Ricky and everyone else drew in a deep breath. What could have happened?

"Unfortunately, last night we lost Mrs Wilson."

Everyone gasped in shock. Someone started to weep at the back of the hall.

The biker lady continued, "She was playing hide-and-seek with her family, but her hiding place this time is just too good and she simply can't be found. Until she is, I am acting as her replacement. My name is Mrs Schofield. But you call me Miss, The Schofatron, The

Schofinator, or whatever you like, really."

Ricky looked at Simon, who was slowly removing his visor.

"The Schofatron is cool," Ricky whispered.

She looked to the door and gave a wave with her hand. "Come in, Spencer. Don't be shy."

A boy Ricky's age, with sandy hair and lots of freckles, shuffled into the hall, barely lifting his eyes.

"This is my son, Spencer," said Mrs Schofield. "We've just moved to the area, so I hope you'll all make him welcome. He'll be in Mr Pinkerton's class."

Spencer looked up briefly, casting a glance for somewhere to sit. On the front row, Vince called, "Here's a spot next to me."

Ricky frowned. Normally Vince was about as friendly as a rattlesnake. Spencer walked over, and the next moment cried "Argh!", as his feet shot from beneath him.

"Oops," said Vince, chuckling. "Must've been a wet spot."

"Right," said Mrs Schofield. "Enjoy your day, guys. I have only one rule, and I'll come down hard if you break it. That rule is . . . have fun!"

The whole assembly broke into applause.

Apart from Mr Pinkerton. He was shifting uncomfortably, like he *really* wanted to let rip with a good trump. Stinkerton loved rules, so the idea of there only being *one* would not please him AT ALL.

As everyone stood up to leave for their next lesson, Ricky went over to Spencer. He offered him his left hand. "Stick with us," he said. "My name's Ricky and this is Simon."

Spencer smiled gratefully and shook Ricky's hand. Vince muttered, "Creep," under his breath.

"Tell you what," said Mrs Schofield as they walked towards the doors. "Let's not bother with your next lesson. Go outside and play instead. Fresh air is good for you."

Everyone looked at each other in shock and then cheered. Ricky started running for the doors to the playground.

A hand dropped on to his shoulder. He turned to see Mr Pinkerton. "Forgotten something, Mitre? You've got lines to do."

Ricky's heart sank as he watched the other kids run out into the sunshine.

CHAPTER 2
COPYCATS

Ricky could still hear their shouts of joy as he was writing his fifth line. At least he didn't have to stand on a stool to reach the top of the board any more. Ever since *that* toilet-cleaning incident, Ricky Mitre had a special power that only a few people knew about.

When he heard footsteps coming, he tucked his arm away.

It was only Simon.

"Hey, mate," he said, winking, "I've got a plan to break you out," and he hurried over to his school bag.

"I don't think that's wise," said Ricky. "If I don't write my lines, Stinkerton's bum will turn into a lethal weapon."

"Wait and see," said Simon. He undid the zip on his bag and took out a cardboard tube. Popping off the top, he slid out what looked like a stack of metal rulers. He flicked a switch, and the whole thing unfolded into a large frame of interlocking pieces.

"What is it?" said Ricky.

"I call it 'the Copytron'," said Simon. "I invented it. It's a device used for copying. Watch!"

Simon took the weird contraption over to the board, and fastened several board pens into different slots. He wrote *Mathematics nourishes the mind*, and as if by magic, the same thing appeared in several rows below.

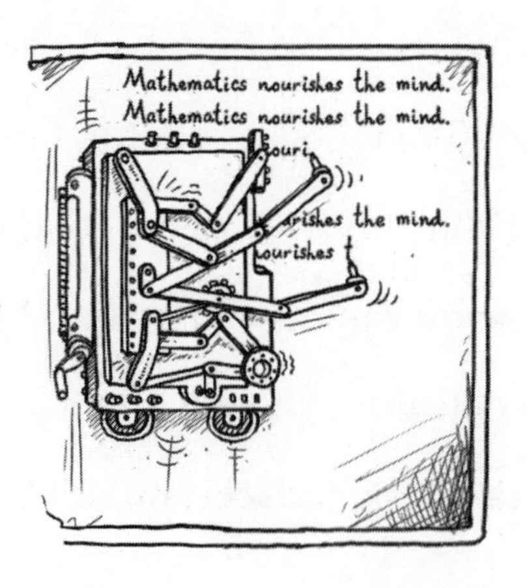

"Awesome!" said Ricky. "Simon, you're like Einstein, Archimedes and Quasimodo all rolled into one!"

Simon frowned. "Thanks, but I haven't got a hunchback."

"Einstein had a hunchback?" asked Ricky.

Simon just shook his head.

"The point is," said Ricky, "I'll be able to do my lines ten times as quickly."

Indeed, two minutes later, Ricky was walking on to the schoolyard. Mr Pinkerton was eating cold baked beans out of the tin. When he saw Ricky, he squinted. "What are you doing outside?"

"Lines done," said Ricky, proudly.

"Go and check."

"Oh, I will," said Mr Pinkerton, wiping bean juice from his chin.

As soon as he was gone, Ricky heard the sound of Vince's voice. "Hey, Spencer, catch!"

Through a crowd, Ricky saw Spencer. He was wandering round blindly, with his school tie covering his eyes. His hands scrabbled to untie the knot as a football hit him in the back of the head. Vince took aim again. "Close!" he said. "Try one more time."

Oof! The football hit him in the stomach.

Ricky's skin tingled. He wouldn't stand for this.

"Wait!" said Simon, as if sensing Ricky's anger. "You can't go up against Vince. He eats rocks for breakfast and bench-presses Year Ones."

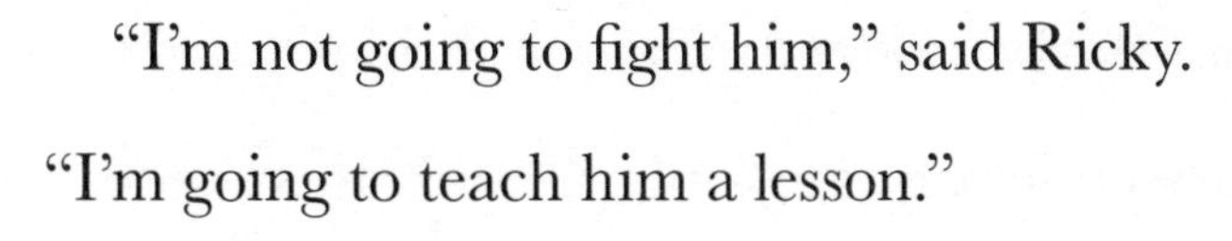

"I'm not going to fight him," said Ricky. "I'm going to teach him a lesson."

All eyes were on poor Spencer, so Ricky let his arm unfurl from under his top, and snaked it through the crowd. He reached for Vince's

trousers and unfastened his belt. Vince was wearing a pair of boxer shorts decorated with pink unicorns.

As he hopped away, everyone laughed. Ricky went to Spencer and helped untie the blindfold.

"Thanks again," said Spencer. "It's always like this when your mum's a teacher. I hate it."

"But your mum is awesome," said Ricky.

Spencer shrugged. "I guess so." He hesitated, blushing. "Listen, can I sit next to you in class?"

Ricky thought about Simon briefly. They *always* sat together, and had since they first came to school. But Spencer was new – he had no friends.

"Sure," said Ricky.

Simon would understand.

*

Simon did not understand.

"But we always sit together," he said.

"It's just for a few days," said Ricky. "Till Spencer settles in."

"OK," said Simon. Then he lowered his voice. "You should be careful – using your arm like that in the open."

"No one saw," said Ricky, feeling annoyed. He'd only done it to help Spencer. "I know what I'm doing."

Simon looked like he was going to argue, but in the end he just said, "Are we still on for lunchtime?"

"Of course," said Ricky.

*

The next lesson was history. The topic was Ancient Egypt, so Mr Pinkerton was showing the class pictures of the pyramids, Tutankhamen and then a weird-looking statue of a cat. Mr Pinkerton let out a very high-pitched squeal (and almost a trump).

The class began to laugh.

Everyone in the school knew of Mr Pinkerton's hatred for cats but no one knew why. Rumours had gone around for years about the possible reasons.

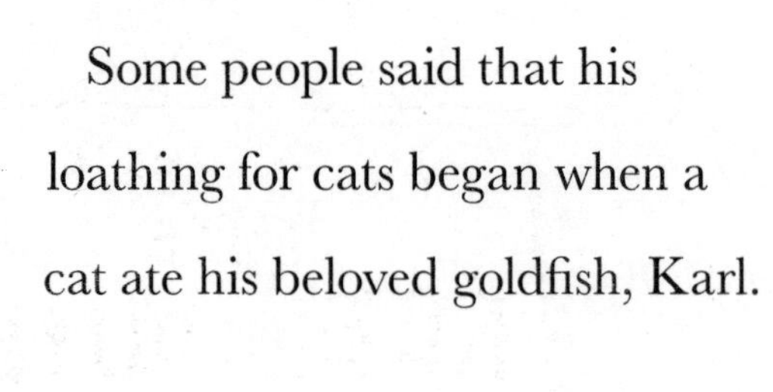

Some people said that his loathing for cats began when a cat ate his beloved goldfish, Karl.

Others said that when he was little the next-door neighbour's cat stole his bike.

There's one other rumour too, but it's so ridiculous. The rumour is that Mr Pinkerton once married a cat, but the cat ran off with the postman. But like I say, that's ridiculous – I mean who would ever marry Mr Pinkerton?

When the lunch bell went, Ricky gave Simon a nod, and they left the classroom. Instead of joining the lunch queue, they veered off into the direction of Mr Smears's broom cupboard.

Ricky was about to knock, when a voice at his back said, "You not coming to lunch?"

It was Spencer. "Sorry, I can't," said Ricky. "Things to do."

Spencer looked at him pleadingly.

"You'll be fine on your own," said Simon, patting him on the shoulder. "Just don't touch the mashed potato. Chef bulks it up with his own hair."

When Spencer had drifted off with the rest of the school to the canteen, Ricky did his secret knock.

Tap-Tap-Tappity... Pause... *Tap.*

"Enter," said a gruff voice.

Ricky opened the door and they entered. It was gloomy inside, lit only by a faint shade-less light bulb hanging from the ceiling. There were shelves with paint pots and overalls and tools. The air was thick with dust. As his eyes slowly adjusted, Ricky made out the caretaker, Mr Smears. He was reading a magazine called *50 Sheds in Grey (And Other Colours).*

"Go right down," he said.

Ricky went to a set of shelves. On the top one, way out of reach without a ladder, was a dusty thermos flask.

“Ready?” he said to Simon.

Simon nodded, and stood next to him.

As soon as Ricky touched the lid, it glowed green. “Fingerprints accepted,” said a soft electronic voice. Ricky turned the lid a full circle, and with a soft click, a portion of the floor dropped away. Ricky and Simon plummeted so fast Ricky felt his stomach trying to escape through his throat.

CHAPTER 3
LONG ARM'S LAIR

THUD!

It stopped. Ricky stepped out of the elevator into a room lit by strip lights. There were work desks littered with pieces of wiring and machinery, and a wall of monitors linked to every CCTV camera in Wolvesley.

They had Mr Smears to thank for the lab. He'd told them that there were a series of tunnels running beneath the school, and

Simon had kitted it out with all the latest technology. It even had Wi-Fi.

The first thing Ricky did, as always when he got down to the lab, was to give his arm a good stretch. Then he began to repair his suit with a needle and thread. It had been badly ripped in the incident at the garden centre with the exploding cacti.* Simon, meanwhile, went behind a screen. Ricky heard a series of clangs and curses.

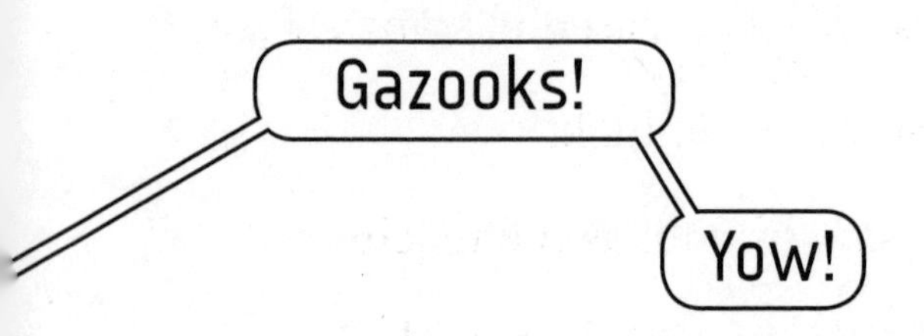

* Don't ask.

"What are you doing?" he asked.

"Inventing," said Simon.

Ricky went back to stitching. He was still thinking about what Simon had said about not using his arm for little things. Perhaps his pal was right. Or maybe he was just jealous.

"Get ready!" said Simon from behind the screen.

Ricky thought he was ready, but when Simon emerged he practically jumped out of his seat. His friend was encased in some sort of robot, towering seven feet high.

"Meet ED," said Simon, as the machine stomped towards Ricky. It held out a hand.

"Er, hi, ED," he said, taking the hand.

The metal fingers squeezed and Ricky felt the bones of his hand crush together. "Ouch!" he cried. "Stop!"

Simon released him. "Oops – sorry. Still adjusting the power controls."

Ricky rubbed his sore hand. "Why 'ED'?"

"Exoskeleton Droid," said Simon proudly. "He's programmed in combat arts, and can lift weights of up to 200 kilos. And he can fly. Watch."

Simon pressed a couple of buttons and ED's foot shot up in a high kick stopping a whisker short of Ricky's chin. "Cool!" said Ricky.

"And he's got a nunchuck attachment," said Simon. ED opened a compartment in his leg and drew out two batons connected with a chain. He spun them in dizzying arcs in front of Ricky's face.

"Double cool!" said Ricky.

"And he has a samurai mode."

ED reached over his shoulder. Ricky stepped back, expecting a deadly sword. Instead, ED was holding a mop.

Simon frowned.

"Sorry!" called down Mr Smears. "I borrowed him a couple of times."

That night, Ricky opened his front door quietly, and tiptoed to the stairs. His mum always wanted to know about his test results, but if he just managed to get upstairs, perhaps there was a chance...

"Hi, sweet pea!" said his mum, coming out of the kitchen. "How did you do in that maths test?"

"Er... Ah... Good," said Ricky.

"Good as in a B?" asked his mum.

"Good as in a W," said Ricky.

His mum pursed her lips. "Is a W good?"

"It's better than an X, Y or Z," said Ricky.

His mum grimaced. "Oh, Ricky. Are we going to have to talk to your teacher again? It took for ever to get that whiff out of my cardy last time."

Ricky shrugged. "He's not smelly any more, but yeah, he might want a chat."

They were both silent for a moment, contemplating Mr Pinkerton's lack of pong. Ricky heard the sounds from the kitchen radio.

"*...speculation that Long Arm is actually an alien from the planet Skidillybop. Professor U. Ranus, Head Stargazer at the*

Agency For All Things Spacey, has told this show that the chance we are alone in the universe is vanishingly small..."

Ricky grinned. They thought he was an alien – like Superman!

"I don't know what you've got to smile about, young man," said his mum. "Maybe if you apply yourself at school, you could be admired like Long Arm one day."

Ricky wiped the smile off his face and nodded. "I hope so, Mum."

"Now go and walk the dog before dinner, please," she said. "His lead is in Scarlett's room."

"Can't she walk him?" asked Ricky.

"No – she's got a spot and won't go out," said his mum.

Ricky plodded upstairs to get changed, with Elliot jumping at his heels. On the way to his room, Ricky saw his older sister's bedroom door was open. The sign on the door read:

He peered in and found her sitting with a bag over her head. "Go away, Mum!" she sobbed.

"It's me," said Ricky. "Have you seen Elliot's lead?"

"On the chest of drawers," she said.

As Ricky went over, he noticed a new poster on her wall. It showed Long Arm cuddling a kitten.

"Long Arm's pretty cool, isn't he?" said Ricky.

"What would you know, loser?" said Scarlett. "Now scram."

Ricky used to hate walking Elliot, especially the bit where he had to pick up the poo. With his long arm, though, he didn't really have to get that close.

He didn't have to do much walking either. In fact, he sat on a bench in a quiet spot and listened to the new Desert Penguins album, while Elliot scampered into bushes, through a wood and into some nice fields.

But after half an hour, Ricky noticed something strange. Elliot wasn't pulling on the lead any more. And then he found out why.

Elliot had gone!

"ELLIOT!" Ricky called. "Here, boy!"

He shouted until his voice was hoarse. He whistled until his lips were dry. He walked in circles, in squares, and even in a dodecahedron, but he couldn't find Elliot anywhere. So, eventually, he went home. Perhaps Elliot would be there.

He wasn't.

"But how could you lose him?" asked his dad. "The lead is only five feet long!"

Ricky didn't know what to say, but he felt dreadful.

BRING ME THE DOG!
In with the others.
I'll have Long Arm's secret soon ... and then I'll be unstoppable.
HA HA HA HA HA HA...

CHAPTER 4
STAMPEDE!

Ricky didn't sleep well. He kept thinking he could hear Elliot barking at the back door, but every time he got up to check, there was nothing there.

"You look terrible!" said Simon, as he arrived the next day to walk to school. "Too much **Barry the Hedgehog**?"

Ricky told his friend what had happened. "I lost Elliot out walking," he said.

"How come?" asked Simon.

Ricky couldn't bring himself to say it was because he was being lazy and using his arm. "He must have slipped out of his collar."

"That's rotten luck," said Simon. "I'm sure he'll be home before you know it. Do you think Mrs Wilson will come out of hiding soon?"

"I hope not," said Ricky. "The Schofinator is awesome."

"Quite. Do you think there's something a bit . . . weird about her?" asked Simon.

"Yeah," said Ricky. "She's cool!"

"Exactly," said Simon. "She barely even seems like a real teacher."

They were just walking through the middle of town when the ground below Ricky's feet started to shake.

"Earthquake!" cried a shopkeeper.

Ricky struggled to balance as the shaking got worse and worse. Then he saw what was causing the earth to move.

Charging down the street were three hippopotamuses.

People scattered in a panic and cars veered into each other trying get away. The hippos flattened several market stalls as they ran this way and that. And now they were heading straight for an elderly coach party who had just got off the Wolvesley Sightseeing Tour.

"They must have escaped from the zoo!" said Simon. "Quick, we have to do something!"

He turned to Ricky, but Ricky was gone.

Telephone

Ten seconds later. . .

"It's Long Arm,"

cried the shopkeeper. "He's

here to save us!"

Ricky looked at the onrushing hippos, then at the coach party. They'd be squished flat as geriatric pancakes if he didn't do something, and fast. But how could he stop three stampeding hippos?

There was only one way.

Tripwire!

Ricky shot out his long arm, gripping a lamp post across the street. He squeezed hard – determined not to let go.

The hippos ran straight into his arm. The

first went somersaulting over the top, looking as surprised as a hippo can. The second tripped and slid along the pavement.

But the third jumped the arm like it was in the 100 metre hurdles Olympic final and continued on its way.

Finally the coach party saw what was coming.

"Is this part of the tour?" said an old man with an ice cream.

"I don't think so," gasped an old woman as her teeth fell out.

Then everyone froze.

Ricky wasted no time. He formed a lasso in the end of his arm and hurled it towards the stray hippo. The loop snagged over its neck and Ricky braced himself. He was yanked off his feet, but even as he was dragged down the road, he didn't let go.

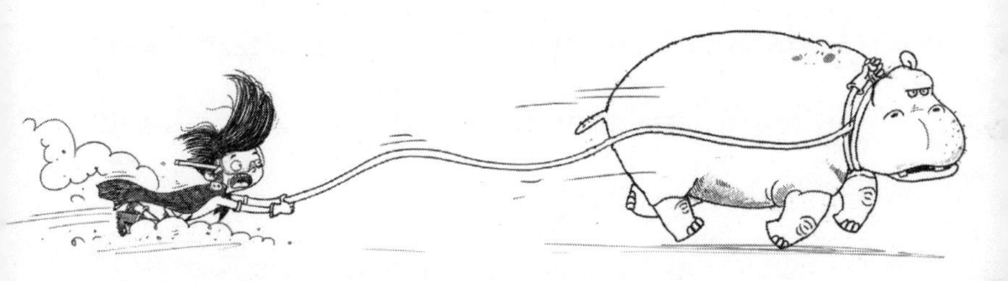

The hippo stopped half a metre short of the coach party, panting heavily. Then it ate the old man's ice cream.

And everyone cheered.

"Long Arm saves the day again!" came a cry.

"Three cheers for Long Arm!" someone else added.

Ricky quickly coiled his arm around all three hippos. "I'd better get them back to the zoo," he said to Simon. "See you at school."

Ricky led the hippos back to Wolvesley Zoo. To his surprise, there weren't any alarms going off, or a commotion of any kind. The gates, however, had seen better days. They were smashed to bits.

He went straight to the head keeper's office, and found him with his feet up, watching a small TV and chuckling.

"Hello?" said Ricky.

"Just a minute," said the keeper, without turning around. "This is going to be good."

Ricky looked at the TV. The zookeeper was watching a rerun of *Britain's Got Flatulence* (or BGF for the hard-core fans). It was the biggest, smelliest show on TV, in which members of the public showed off their ability to trump on cue. Some gave trump renditions of their favourite songs, some tried to trump for the longest amount of time (the current record was three minutes and seven seconds), and some – the real elite – just tried to create the loudest, foulest trump of all time.

On the screen, four little children stood on stage, beaming proudly. A row of judges in chairs were wafting their faces. "That was the smelliest rendition of 'My Heart Will Go On' I've ever smelled," one judge said. The audience cheered.

"I didn't like it," said the head judge. The audience briefly booed, and then he continued, "I LOVED it. You're through to pump camp!"

Finally the zookeeper turned to Ricky. "Nice Long Arm costume!" he said.

"I am Long Arm," said Ricky. "And I brought your hippos back."

The zookeeper didn't appear to hear what Ricky was saying. "I love this show!" he said. "Don't you? I mean – those kids – the talent! The *timing*! They're definitely going to get a bum deal after this."

"I'm more of a Desert Penguins fan," said Ricky. "Anyway . . . the hippos."

"What about them?"

"I brought them back before they squished everyone in Wolvesley."

"Oh, right. Thanks. I wasn't aware they'd escaped. I've been watching this all morning. I suppose we'd better put them back in their pen."

Ricky followed the keeper back to the hippos' enclosure. "Go on in, Louis," he said, patting the first hippo on the bum. "And you, Niall. Yes, Liam, you'll get your food soon." As the third hippo entered the pen, the keeper turned to Ricky. "Where's Harry?"

"Harry?" said Ricky.

"Hippo number four. The naughty one. They've been a foursome ever since Zayne ran off."

"I don't know," said Ricky. "There were only three running down the high street."

The zookeeper sucked a breath through his teeth. "This is happening rather a lot recently."

"What is?"

"Animals going missing."

"Have you reported it to the police?" said Ricky.

"I tried," said the keeper. "But they were watching BGF too. Did you see that woman with the dog? They could trump in time with each other."

"I've got to get to sch— I mean, I've got to go," said Ricky. But as he left the zoo, he began to ponder. Elliott disappearing without a trace, and more animals at the zoo vanishing into thin air. . .

What if it wasn't a coincidence?

CHAPTER 5
HAMSTER BURGLAR

Ricky was late. Very late indeed. He ran straight to the main hall, where Mrs Schofield was taking assembly. It wasn't like one of Mrs Wilson's assemblies, where they talked about the environment, or looking smart, or road safety. In fact, it looked like a motor rally. Mrs Schofield was giving the kids turns on her motorbike.

Ricky walked in and Mr Pinkerton bellowed.

"Mitre! What time do you call this?"

L.O.F.T #197 - Lateness

Katie Locke stopped doing doughnuts on the motorbike and everyone went quiet. Mr Smears went about quietly mopping up oil stains from the floor.

"Sorry, sir," said Ricky. "Would you believe there was a hippo stampede in town?"

"No," said Mr Pinkerton. He gritted his teeth. *Surely he was going to trump now*, Ricky thought. But he didn't. Instead he did a series of breathing exercises, before continuing.

"You know what this means, don't you, Mitre?"

"Lines?" said Ricky.

Mr Pinkerton nodded. "More lines than ever before. And this time you won't have that little device to help you."

Simon blushed.

"Yes, I found it," said Mr Pinkerton.

"No need to punish the boy," said Mrs Schofield, stepping up beside Ricky. "We're all late from time to time."

"But. . ." began Mr Pinkerton.

"Maybe we should cut him some slack?" said Mrs Schofield.

Mr Pinkerton did his breathing again and a very unconvincing smile. "I'm sorry, Mrs Schofield, or Schofie, or whatever you're called. I did a bit of research last night – into your credentials..."

"And?" said the new head.

"*AND*... I couldn't find you listed anywhere. No CV, no teaching history. Isn't that strange?"

Ricky felt the temperature in the room drop to sub-zero as the two teachers eyeballed each other.

Mrs Schofield shrugged. "Must be an administrative error."

"Indeed," hissed Mr Pinkerton. He pointed a stubby finger at Mrs Schofield, and the sweat patches dripped under his arms. "I'll be keeping an eye on you," he said. Then he stormed out of the hall.

After he'd gone, Mrs Schofield smiled. She wafted her hand in front of her nose. "Someone needs a bath."

All the kids laughed, except for Simon.

"Thanks for sticking up for me!" said Ricky.

Mrs Schofield winked. "If you need anything, Ricky Mitre, just drop by my office. All right?"

"Sure," said Ricky.

"Now," said Mrs Schofield. "I'm afraid I have some bad news. Last night, a burglar entered the school."

All the kids gasped.

"Only one thing was taken, and that was George, the school hamster. We don't have a culprit as yet, but it's clear that the school can't have been properly locked. For that reason, I'm announcing the immediate dismissal of Mr Smears, the caretaker, for gross negligence."

Mr Smears looked up. "Pardon?"

"I'm sorry," said Mrs Schofield. "The school board took the decision. I'm just the messenger. Leave the mop by the door on your way out."

Mr Smears's shoulders drooped and he shuffled out of the hall.

Ricky watched him go, speechless. Mr Smears had been at the school *for ever.* Rumour had it his family had been caretakers since the Middle Ages.

"Assembly over," said Mrs Schofield. "Off you go, and remember: have fun!"

On the way out of the hall, Ricky sidled up to Simon. "Mr Smears always locks the doors," he said. "He can't be to blame."

"I know," said Simon. "And can the school board really have met this morning?"

"I guess not," said Ricky. "Do you think Mrs Schofield is lying?"

Simon narrowed his eyes. "I don't like this at all."

"Like what?" said Spencer, appearing between them.

"None of your business," said Simon.

Spencer looked hurt, and wandered off.

"You shouldn't be so mean to him," said Ricky. "He's just trying to be friends."

"I don't want to be his friend," said Simon. "I don't like him. Or his mum. There's something not *right* about them."

Ricky stopped by the vending machine. "Hang on, I want to get a can of Orange Ade."

"It's been banned in twelve countries across the EU," said Simon. "They did tests and found it was half industrial cleanser."

"Yeah, but it makes your eyes glow orange for up to three hours," said Ricky.

"Is that a good thing?" said Simon.

"Is it a bad thing?" said Ricky. Orange Ade was also the secret ingredient that had made his arm grow long, but no one else knew that.

He put his money in the slot, before he saw there was no Orange Ade left. "Strange," he said. "I thought I was the only person who drank it."

On the way back to class, Ricky told Simon about the missing animals at the zoo. "What if it's all connected? The hamster, the hippo and Elliott?"

Simon did his thinking face. "We need to get down to the lab," he said. "If we analyse all the data maybe we can find a pattern to help us catch the animal-napper."

"Good thinking," said Ricky. "There might be something caught on the cameras too."

While all the other kids went out to play, Ricky and Simon went back to Mr Smears's cupboard. Or simply a cupboard, as it now was. Ricky didn't bother to knock this time, and just pushed open the door. Inside was Mrs Schofield.

She looked up, shocked.

"Oh, hello you two!" she said. "I was just doing an inventory. Looking for something?"

Ricky thought fast. "Um . . . spare toilet rolls!" he said. "We've run out in the boys' toilets."

Mrs Schofield pointed to a shelf. "Well, there they are," she said.

Ricky took one, and felt Mrs Schofield

watching every step. He saw the thermos was still on the shelf. There was no chance she could find the lab though – not without a ladder.

At least he hoped not.

LATER THAT NIGHT...
ORANGE
This is the key - I'm sure of it! Bring out the next test subject.
Come on! Don't let me down!
Open the door! Let me see! ...
NOOOOOOOOO!
We can try again. There must be another ingredient.
I'VE WAITED LONG ENOUGH! We need Long Arm's DNA. And I know just how we can get it.

CHAPTER 6
HANGING BY A THREAD

When the school bell rang for the end of the day, and the other kids were walking home, Ricky and Simon were in the lab. Sure enough, nothing had been disturbed. Their secret was safe.

They sat at the bank of monitors that hacked into every security camera in Wolvesley. It was painstaking work reviewing hours of footage.

Most of the cameras were working fine,

but the ones that covered the docks were all malfunctioning. Ricky focused on the school. He saw Mr Smears leaving at the end of the previous day, locking the doors behind him.

"I knew it!" he said.

Then he wound the tape forward until another figure sped into view. It was blurry footage, but the guy was wearing a hoodie. He reached the school doors, and fiddled with the locks. Then he was in.

"Wow – he's quick with a lock pick," said Simon. "Looks like a pro."

Ricky watched the clock roll. Two minutes later, out he came again. There was a bulge in his pocket.

"That's enough to prove it wasn't Mr Smears," said Ricky. "But there's no way we can identify the real culprit from that."

"Uh-oh!" said Simon. He was pointing at a different screen. "We've got an emergency." A camera panned across the centre of Wolvesley. Ricky saw the statue of Long Arm proudly standing in the town square. And there was a figure, hanging from the top of the quiff.

"Zoom in!" he said.

Simon twisted a dial, and Ricky saw the figure was a boy. Spencer! He was dangling by his fingertips, his face full of fear.

"How did he get up there?" said Simon.

"Maybe Vince and his pals?" said Ricky. "We've got to rescue him."

"Be careful!" said Simon. "That hippo is still on the loose. Maybe you should leave it to the fire brigade."

"They won't get there in time," said Ricky, already donning his Long Arm suit.

He ran across the lab, to where an oil-stained sheet lay draped over a workbench.

He whipped it off, to reveal the Vecta3000. Wondering what that is? Well, it was a skateboard, with some rockets attached.

Ricky climbed on. "Light me up!"

Simon lit the rockets, and Ricky shot off through the tunnel.

He emerged by the sports pavilion in the school fields, then steered the Vecta3000 through the streets of Wolvesley, until he arrived at the town square.

"Help me!" cried Spencer. "I'm going to fall."

"Don't panic!" called Ricky. "Long Arm is here."

A crowd had gathered around the bottom of the statue, and Ricky pushed his way through. He reached up his arm, letting it uncoil and loop over the statue's shoulder until his hand was hanging down the other side.

"You'll have to let go!" he shouted. "Take my hand."

Spencer looked down, beads of sweat

pouring off his forehead.

"I can't!"

"Do it!" said Ricky. "Trust me!"

Then Spencer's fingers slipped and he plummeted.

All of Wolvesley watched in horror.

Ricky stretched his arm, and snagged Spencer's belt just before he hit the ground.

All of Wolvesley cheered.

And then went about their business.

They were getting used to Long Arm's heroics.

Ricky led Spencer away from the statue to a quiet spot on a bench.

"Thank you!" said Spencer. "You saved me, Long Arm!"

Ricky thought he sounded a bit sad.

"No problem," he replied. "But how did you even get up there?"

Spencer blushed. "I'm sorry," he said.

"Why are you sorry?" said Ricky.

"For this," said Spencer. Ricky saw he was holding something in his hand. It was a brown canvas bag. He lifted it above Ricky's head.

Then everything went black.

Where am I?

I've got him!

Good work. Exactly according to plan.

Are you sure this is the only way?

Now isn't the time for doubts.

I know, but...

No buts. The days of Long Arm are over.

Take off the bag...

CHAPTER 7

A PAIN IN THE NECK

Bright lights blinded Ricky.

He was lying face-up, and when he tried to move, he realized his arms and legs were tied.

Gradually, squinting, he made out a vast windowless room. He was on a table. He managed to turn his head, and the first thing he saw was a motorbike.

"Wakey, wakey!" said a voice he recognized.

Mrs Schofield stood over him. "Take off his mask," she said.

“Maybe we shouldn’t,” said Spencer’s voice.

“Don’t you want to know who the mysterious Long Arm really is?” she replied.

“No!” mumbled Ricky.

But Spencer appeared, hooked his fingers under the mask and pulled it off.

“Ricky Mitre!” he said.

“Of course it’s young Mitre!” said Mrs Schofield. “Couldn’t you even work that out, silly boy? The four-foot-tall boy who can suddenly score twenty slam dunks in a basketball match. . . The lateness at school timed perfectly with superheroics in Wolvesley. . . The grades plummeting almost as fast as Long Arm's fame grows. . ."

Spencer was pale with shock.

"What's going on?" said Ricky. "Let me go!"

Mrs Schofield smiled. It was the same smile she'd used in assembly, only instead of looking sweet and nice, it now looked like the sort of smile a crocodile might give you if you happened to stick your head into its pen at the zoo.

"I've been following you," said Mrs

Schofield. “Ever since Long Arm hit the news, I’ve wanted to know your secret.”

“You took the Orange Ade, didn’t you?” he said.

“You might not know it, but Orange Ade contains Plutonium six, a rare ingredient known for stretching molecules.”

“And it tastes great!” said Spencer.

“You really shouldn’t drink it,” said his mother. “Plutonium six was used by the Russians for fuelling rockets in the sixties.”

"The animals – that was you too, wasn't it?" said Ricky.

"I heard you were no good at maths, Mitre. But at last you've put two and two together!"

"And Spencer was just bait!"

"Which you swallowed hook, line and sinker!"

Ricky fought against the bonds, but couldn't move.

Mrs Schofield looked up and down his arm. "Such power!" she said. "And now it will be mine." She took out a pair of scissors.

"Are you going to try and cut my arm off with a pair of scissors?" said Ricky. "I really don't think that will work."

"No, you idiot!" she said. "Not yet, anyway." She came closer, then took his hand in hers and with a quick *snip,* cut off a sliver on his fingernail. She walked quickly across the room to what looked like a giant metal egg. "I just need your DNA," she said. She pressed a switch and a panel slid back. She laid the piece of nail inside and the panel closed again. "My machine will analyse your biological make-up, and I will replicate your power. Soon I will be Long Arm, and I will rule the world!"

"Er. . . how will a long arm let you rule the world?" said Ricky.

"Shut up!" screeched Mrs Schofield. "Do not question my evilness."

"What will you do with Ricky?" said Spencer.

"I haven't decided yet," said his mother. "Rest assured, it will be . . . messy."

"But he's my friend," said Spencer.

Mrs Schofield rolled her eyes. "You don't need friends, Spencer. Soon you will be a prince in my empire."

"Again," interrupted Ricky. "Not sure you've completely thought this through. . ."

"Enough!" said Mrs Schofield. "The time has come."

She opened the door to the egg-shaped pod, and stepped inside. As she closed the door behind her, lights flashed over the surface.

"What's she doing?" asked Ricky.

Spencer just swallowed.

Back in the lab, Simon was wondering where Ricky had got to. He'd watched the rescue at the statue on the monitors, then gone back to sifting the footage looking for missing animals. And at last, he found something.

It came from the zoo camera focused on the ape enclosure. It showed someone sneaking inside, and bundling up a chimpanzee. At first Simon couldn't tell who is was, but then he recognized the shoes. Biker boots.

"It's Mrs Schofield!" he gasped.

But why was she stealing animals?

*

"Why's she stealing animals?" asked Ricky.

"Experimentation," Spencer replied. "She's wanted your secret from the start, but she didn't want to test on herself."

Ricky's veins flooded with anger. Elliot ... what had she done to him?

In the lab, Simon tried calling Ricky again on their communicators. No answer.

He went back to the footage from the rescue. He saw Ricky lead Spencer away. A horrible feeling dawned over him, like someone pouring iced water into his underpants.

"If Mrs Schofield was bad. . ."

He swapped cameras and found Long Arm and Spencer on a bench together. They were talking. Then . . . what was that? A hood!

Simon watched as Ricky toppled over. A few seconds later a motorbike cruised into view, ridden by Mrs Schofield. Spencer helped load Ricky's limp body across the seat. Then they sped away.

But where was she taking him? Simon scanned all the monitors. No sign of the bike, Mrs Schofield or anything suspicious. Which meant they'd gone to the only place the cameras were down.

"The docks!" said Simon.

*

As the fizzes and pops ended, the pod was glowing orange from all the Orange Ade. The door opened with a hiss and orange smoke billowed out. Spencer was trembling.

A single arm emerged from the smoke.

Then another.

Both were normal length. Ricky breathed a sigh of relief. It hadn't worked.

Then Mrs Schofield staggered out.

Something was wrong.

She had no head. Or rather, her neck didn't end in a head. It ended in more neck. She walked out, and with every step another foot of neck was revealed.

"What's happening?" she said, her voice coming from inside the pod. Her feet stumbled and tripped as though she couldn't see where she was going, and still her neck unravelled. Spencer leapt back as she lumbered aimlessly towards them.

Then, finally, her head appeared.

"Oh dear," she said.

Simon shot across the sky in his ED costume. His on-board systems analysed trajectories and windspeeds, satellite movement and traffic flow. And, of course, Twitter.

"One minute until destination," said the suit calmly.

Simon angled down, heading straight for the warehouses that lined the dockside. Mrs

Schofield was there somewhere.

And so was his friend.

"Mum?" said Spencer. "Are you OK?"

Mrs Schofield's head shot down to face him.

"Never better!" she said. Her neck wobbled around like a melted cheese stick. "Just getting my bearings."

"Why is your neck long instead of your arm?"

"I have no idea," she replied. "But this won't stop me. Wolvesley will still be mine. And then, the world!" She switched on a TV screen. *Britain's Got Flatulence* was on.

For a second Mrs Schofield forgot what she was meant to be doing and instead starting watching the greatest TV show in the world.

She quickly snapped out of it and switched over the twenty-four-hour Wolvesley news channel, which showed Sammy Sammerson fast asleep with his head on his news desk. "You'll have a prime view. . ."

Ricky pleaded with his teacher. "Please, Mrs Schofield. Don't do this!"

Mrs Schofield glowered at him. "Quiet!" she shouted. "I am no longer Mrs Schofield, I . . . am Long Neck."

She began to laugh uncontrollably, violently throwing her head from side to side

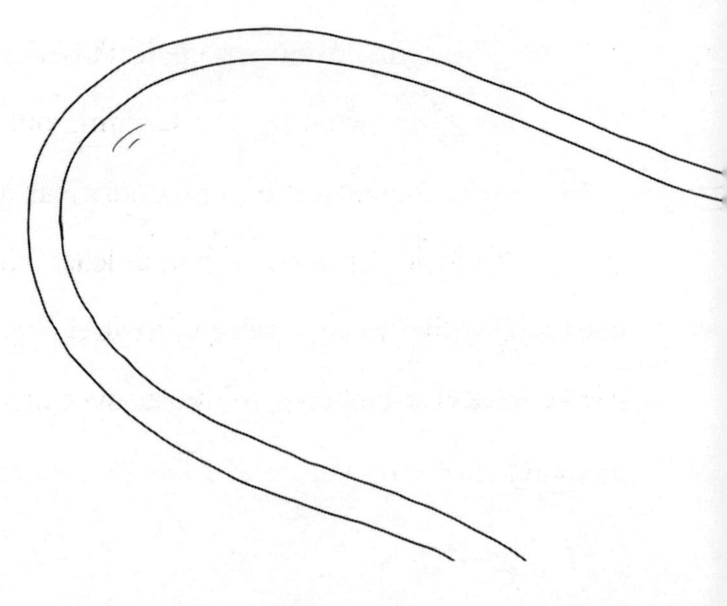

like the Loch Ness Monster thrashing in the water.

"Spencer, you make sure he stays exactly where he is."

Then she marched right out of the door, banging her head on the way.

Simon couldn't believe what he saw. Coming out of one of warehouse doors was Mrs Schofield. Or most of her, at least. Her neck looked like stringy piece of melted cheese, stretched and stretched until it was over fifty feet long.

"Arm missiles!" he said.

ED locked on target.

"Fire!"

The twin missiles scorched through the air towards Mrs Schofield. Her neck contorted into an S shape, and both missed, exploding in the water behind.

"Glad you could join me!" said Mrs Schofield, suddenly right in Simon's ear. He felt something tightening around his middle.

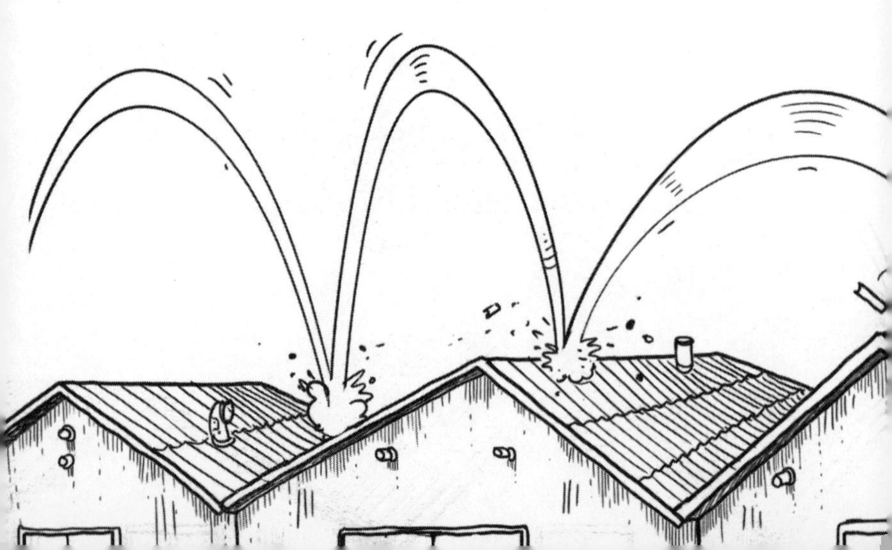

She'd clutched him in the coils of her neck.

Then she hurled him across the warehouse rooftops.

CHAPTER 8
LONG NECK ON THE RAMPAGE

"Welcome to *The Wolvesley Hour*. I'm Sammy Sammerson, wide awake for once. This just in... We have reports of a sighting of a mystery creature reaching enormous heights down at the Wolvesley docks. More on this as we get it. . ."

Mrs Schofield marched into the centre of Wolvesley. "Kneel, my subjects!" she boomed.

But no one heard her, because she was too high up.

And that only made Mrs Schofield angrier!

She headbutted a couple of seagulls out of the sky, just because she could.

"You're listening to Wolvesley FM where we guarantee to make your ears smile. I'm Clare Waves. I'm interrupting the Desert Penguins to bring you news that a new threat faces our town. She's being dubbed Long Neck and right now she's breathing on the highest windows in town and writing naughty messages. The question on everyone's lips... Where is Long Arm? Where is our saviour?"

"Spencer, you have to let me go!" said Ricky, as he watched the news footage of the poor seagulls. "I'm the only one who can stop her."

"I . . . I can't," said Spencer. "She'll go mad."

"I think that boat might have sailed," said Ricky. "Hate to break it to you, Spence, but your mum's bonkers. She just ate a pigeon."

"She's just misguided," said Spencer.

"Well, she's going to hurt innocent people," said Ricky.

Spencer swallowed. "But . . . she's my mum."

"Then you need to help her," said Ricky. "Help me, and I can stop her before the Air Force scrambles fighter jets to shoot her down."

Spencer's eyes went wide. "Would they do that?"

Ricky nodded.

Spencer took the scissors and snipped off the ropes tying Ricky down.

Just as he'd finished, the door burst inwards. Simon stood there, in his ED suit.

He ran straight at Spencer, brandishing Mr Smears's mophead like a sword.

"You'll pay for this!" he cried.

Spencer cowered as the mop came down with brutal force.

Ricky caught ED's hand just in time.

"Spencer's on our side. We need to work together," said Ricky. "All three of us." Even though Simon was angry, he trusted his best friend. "OK," he said. "Let's stop her."

"First, where's Elliot?" said Ricky. He grabbed his mask and tied it back in place.

"Follow me," said Spencer.

*

Meanwhile, back at home, Mr Pinkerton was making some final preparations.

Tonight was a big night for Ricky's teacher. The regional auditions for *Britain's Got Flatulence* were taking place in the local theatre in just a couple of hours. His moment was coming.

The previous weeks had been hard. Normally Mr Pinkerton would trump about a dozen times a day. He took pride in the wrinkled faces of the children as his invisible clouds of foulness collided with their nostrils.

But not any more. Because Mr Pinkerton had not trumped for close to two weeks. He was taking his training very seriously indeed.

Eating the right food – lentils, beans, raw eggs and the mouldiest blue cheese he could find – all designed to produce the worst bottom-burp in the history of mankind. Or animal-kind. The most poisonous gas ever produced.

He would be a star.

Sometimes he woke up sweating, his stomach in knots of pain, just begging for the release. But each time he fought back, keeping the build-up of gas inside.

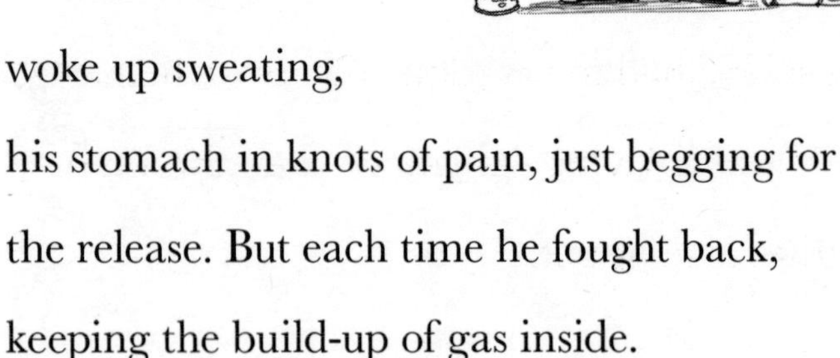

He couldn't wait to see the looks on the judge's faces – if they managed to stay conscious. Fame and *fart*une awaited.

Mr Pinkerton was just about to leave the house when he caught a glimpse of the TV. Every channel was showing the breaking news of Long Neck causing havoc in Wolvesley.

"Mrs Schofield!" he said. "I knew she was a bad egg!"

Mr Pinkerton shook his head in disgust, switched off the TV and rushed out of the house. He had to get to the theatre, whether there was a raving, long-necked madwoman on the loose or not.

*

Spencer led Ricky and Simon down a dark corridor. Ricky was terrified at what he might find. If Mrs Schofield had hurt Elliot, he would be devastated.

"None of the experiments quite worked," Spencer said. "She never got the right mixture of ingredients."

Spencer flicked a light switch, and a number of lamps lit up a row of cages.

Ricky walked past them slowly. He saw a bald hamster, a blue-and-green striped chimpanzee, a hippo with wings,

and a cat on two legs, skipping with a rope. He saw a pigeon doing a Rubix cube, and a brown bear levitating in the lotus position. With every step, he wondered what on earth he would find next.

Last of all, he came to a dog sitting in the middle of the cage, tail wagging happily and tongue lolling.

"Elliot?" he said.

His dog looked completely unharmed. Normal. Ricky's heart sang.

"He's fine," said Ricky. "Not bald, no wings in sight, perfectly normal."

Spencer looked at Ricky with a guilty face and said, "Not quite normal."

"Hello, old chap," said the dog. "Any chance we could leave this dreadful place?"

Ricky stood in silent shock.

"Cat got your tongue, my good man?" said Elliot. "No surprise. But really, it's frightful in here." He pointed with his paw at the bolted door. "If you wouldn't mind?"

Ricky unfastened the bolt, and Elliot padded out.

"Right," said Elliot. "What now?"

"We've got a criminal mastermind to stop,"

said Ricky.

"Lead on!" said Elliot.

"I haven't got your lead," said Ricky.

Elliot cocked his head. "That isn't quite what I . . . Oh, never mind. Proceed!"

CHAPTER 9

LONG ARM VS LONG NECK

"Welcome to *The Wolvesley Hour.* I'm Sammy Sammerson and there's no time for napping. I'm on location in central Wolvesley witnessing extraordinary scenes. Long Neck continues to wreak havoc across town. The army battalion sent to tackle her has proved ultimately useless. . ."

"But who is this? Could it be. . . It is!"

Ricky planted his feet in the street and faced the oncoming tank.

"Stop right there!" he said.

Mrs Schofield laughed from on high. And this time, because she had acquired a megaphone, people could actually hear her. "You can't stop me, Long Arm!"

She aimed the tank's gun turret at Ricky, and pulled the trigger.

BOOM!

Ricky didn't have time to duck. But just as he thought it was the end, something flashed past.

ED!

The cannon's round collided with the

robotic suit, and it spun off in a shower of sparks. It slammed into the leg of the Long Arm statue, smashing it in two, and exploded in a ball of flames.

"Simon!" cried Ricky.

"It's OK!" called Simon, waving from across the street. He waved a little box. "Remote control."

The Long Arm statue teetered precariously.

"How fitting!" cackled Mrs Schofield. "When all this is over, I'll melt that thing down and use the metal to make a new statue. Guess what it will be?"

"A soaring angel?" said Ricky.

"No, guess again."

"A piece of conceptual art representing the futility of existence?"

"Try again."

"One of those big reflective balls that make your reflection squishy?"

Mrs Schofield snarled as she climbed out of the tank. "You're making fun of me, aren't you?"

"Maybe," said Ricky. "Might it be a statue of a long-necked woman?"

"Yes!" said Mrs Schofield. "Now, Long Arm. Let's find out who will rule this town!"

And so they had a . . . Great. Big. Fight.

The whole town took shelter as Long Arm and Long Neck did battle. Buildings fell, roads cracked apart, windows smashed, and the busker who performed out-of-tune Desert Penguins songs even stopped playing.

And at the end of it all. . .

"You're listening to Wolvesley FM where we guarantee to make your ears smile. But today, there are no guarantees. Because, listeners, I bring you grave news. Long Arm has met his match. He lies defeated in the streets of Wolvesley, beneath the statue we erected to honour him. He can barely lift his arm, and we

can hardly bear to watch..."

Ricky looked up to see Mrs Schofield towering over him.

"Mum, don't!" said Spencer, but she didn't listen.

"I knew it would end like this," she said, leaning close. "There's only room for one long-limbed super-being in Wolvesley. And that super-being is. . ."

"Out of my way," said a voice. "Out of my way!"

Ricky saw a man running up the street, seemingly oblivious to the destruction all around.

It was Mr Pinkerton.

Mr Pinkerton slowed down. He looked at Long Arm, then his eyes followed the long, looping coils of Mrs Schofield's neck. His jaw dropped, and his knees wobbled. Then he clutched his stomach. "No, no, no. . ." he said. "Not now."

He began to take short panting breaths, but he knew it was a losing battle.

He crossed his legs, and spun around three times, but each second that passed he knew he couldn't hold it in.

And then it happened.

On the other side of the world, it registered as merely a tremor, but in Wolvesley the trump that detonated from Mr Pinkerton's bottom measured 4.3 on the Richter Scale. It dented the road surface and shattered windows at forty paces. People dived for cover.

And the thing about hot air is, it rises.

So at ground level, the citizens of Wolvesley were spared. Not so Mrs Schofield.

As the green gases rose in a miasma around her, she tried not to breathe. But Mr Pinkerton's trump was of such potency that even the world's most advanced biohazard suit would not have saved her.

In short, she got a lungful.

Her eyes narrowed, and her head tottered. She gasped and wretched and choked. Spasms shook her neck from top to bottom. And then, like a mighty tree, she collapsed.

And all of Wolvesley cheered.

Apart from Elliot the dog. He did a little wee against the remaining leg of the Long Arm statue.

"Don't mind me," said Elliot.

CHAPTER 10

A DISAPPOINTING ENDING

"Welcome to *The Wolvesley Hour*. I'm Sammy Sammerson, and I'm glad to back in the studio after an eventful day. Our town is saved, and the villain known as Long Neck is in custody where she belongs. Goodnight, Wolvesley, and sleep tight...

...

What, we've got another fifty-nine minutes? OK – let's just put up a picture of Long Arm."

In the Mitre household, Scarlett was sitting in the living room with her mum and dad.

"Switch it over!" said her dad. "*Britain's Got Flatulence* is on the other channel."

Mrs Mitre changed the channel, just in time to see a man in a crumpled suit walking on to the stage. His shoulders sagged, and he dragged his feet.

"Hi," said the head judge. "Tell us your name and what you do."

The man looked up nervously. "I'm Mr Pinkerton and I'm a teacher at Wolvesley Primary School."

"Thanks," said the host. "When you're ready."

Mr Pinkerton took a deep breath, then closed his eyes. The audience fell into silence.

After a few seconds, the head judge began tapping his foot.

Mr Pinkerton began to sweat.

"This is going to be massive, I reckon," said Ricky's mum. "Ricky says he trumps all the time at school!"

A tiny whisper came from the vicinity of Mr Pinkerton's bottom.

One audience member clapped. Once. (It was Mr Pinkerton's mum.)

"This guy's a joker," said Ricky's dad.

The judges didn't look impressed.

"Don't give up the teaching just yet," said one.

"Thanks for coming," said another, "but I've heard a mouse trump louder than that."

Mr Pinkerton stalked off the stage.

In Wolvesley Prison, all the prisoners crowded around the TV laughed. All except one.

She was watching the TV, but she was sitting in her cell at the other end of prison.

Mrs Schofield was serving thirty years

for crimes against animals, trying to form a dictatorship and speeding. But she had no intention of spending thirty years behind bars.

She cracked her knuckles, ground her teeth and did 1000 push-ups.

But most of all she thought about Ricky Mitre.

"Outwitted by a schoolboy!" she growled. "Well, you may have won this battle, Long Arm, but I will rise again. . ."

And in Ricky's bedroom, he and Simon were playing **Barry the Hedgehog** while Elliot lay stretched out on the floor.

"Did you get all the animals back to their

original state?" asked Ricky.

"Almost," said Simon. "It was simple really – just reversed the polarity on the sequencing machine, sending a stream of ionized particles through the accelerator. Of course, I had to invent a new form of genetic modelling in order to do so."

"I have no idea what you've just said," replied Ricky. "I had a text from Spencer yesterday."

"How is he?" said Simon.

"Well, considering his mum is an evil criminal mastermind, he's doing OK. He's staying with his Aunty Kath down in Devon."

"That's good to hear," said Simon.

"It's good to have everything back to normal," said Ricky. And he stroked Elliot's head.

Hear, hear. Left a bit, please.